AR Quiz No# 82321
BL# 2.6
AR Pts :0.5

GUS and GRANDPA
and the Piano Lesson

Claudia Mills ★ Pictures by Catherine Stock

Farrar, Straus and Giroux

New York

For Gregory, who asked for this book
—C.M.

For Michael and Juliet
—C.S.

Text copyright © 2004 by Claudia Mills
Illustrations copyright © 2004 by Catherine Stock
All rights reserved
Distributed in Canada by Douglas & McIntyre Ltd.
Color separations by Phoenix Color Corporation
Printed and bound in the United States of America by Phoenix Color Corporation
First edition, 2004
1 3 5 7 9 10 8 6 4 2

www.fsgkidsbooks.com

Library of Congress Cataloging-in-Publication Data
Mills, Claudia.
  Gus and Grandpa and the piano lesson / Claudia Mills ; pictures by Catherine Stock.
    p. cm.
  Summary: After Gus, who would rather play outside than practice music, does not do too
well at his piano recital, his grandfather shows him how music can be fun.
  ISBN 0-374-32814-5
  [1. Piano—Fiction. 2. Music—Fiction. 3. Grandfathers—Fiction. 4. Concerts—
Fiction.] I. Stock, Catherine, ill. II. Title.

PZ7.M63963Gudh 2004
[E]—dc21
                                                                              2002044674

Contents

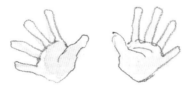

The Longest Half Hour

Gus sat down
on the piano bench.
He opened his music book.

The longest half hour of the day
was the half hour
Gus practiced the piano.

Gus felt hungry.
Maybe he should have
a small snack first.
He got up from the bench
and headed for the kitchen.

"Gus!" his mother called
from upstairs.
"I don't hear anything."

Gus returned to the piano.
He had a new piece to learn.
It was called "The Horse Race."

When he practiced,
Gus's teacher wanted him
to count time out loud.
Gus felt silly doing that.
He counted in his head instead,
except when he forgot
to count at all.

The doorbell rang.
Gus ran with his mother
to answer it.
It was Gus's friend Ryan Mason,
who lived next door.

"Do you want to come over
and shoot some hoops?"
Ryan asked.

"Yes!" Gus shouted.

"Not now," Gus's mother said.
"Gus has to practice the piano."

Gus played "The Horse Race"
over and over again.
His horse kept stopping
and tripping
and falling down.
Gus wished he were playing
basketball instead.

Finally, Gus's half hour was over.
But when he ran outside,
Ryan was gone.

The next day,
Mommy dropped Gus off
at Grandpa's house.
Grandpa was listening
to an opera.
A lady was singing
in a high voice.

Gus didn't like opera.
But Grandpa did.
So did Skipper.
He barked along
with the music.

"How are your
  piano lessons going?"
  Grandpa asked Gus
  when the music stopped.
"They're hard," Gus replied.

"I know,"
  Grandpa said.
"I used to play the violin,
  way back when.
  And your daddy used
  to play the trombone."

The opera started again.
Gus would rather play the piano
than sing in an opera.
But if it were up to him,
he wouldn't do either one.

Squishy Fingers

Gus took his piano lessons
on Thursday afternoons.
Mrs. Moore had a shiny
black grand piano.
She made Gus wash his hands
before he touched the keys.

19

"Look at those fingers!"
Mrs. Moore said
when Gus started playing
"The Horse Race."

Gus looked at his fingers.
Maybe he hadn't scrubbed
them clean enough.

"Are those strong fingers
or squishy fingers?"
Mrs. Moore asked.

Gus took a guess.
"Squishy fingers?"

"And do we want strong fingers
   or squishy fingers?"
Mrs. Moore asked.

Gus took another guess.
"Strong fingers?"
   Mrs. Moore helped Gus
fix his fingers.

Gus played some more
of "The Horse Race."
Mrs. Moore stopped him.
"Did you count out loud
this week, Gus?"

How could she know?
"I counted inside my head,"
Gus said.

"I want you to count *out loud*,"
Mrs. Moore said.
"Your piece is called
'The Horse Race.'
Let's hear your horse
take off at a gallop!"

Gus did his best,
but his horse lost anyway.

"The more you play a piece,
the sooner the music will be
in your fingers,"
Mrs. Moore told Gus.
"Then your horse
will win every race!"

Gus sighed.
He didn't think
that would happen
for a very long time.

The Lost Race

The next month,
Mrs. Moore had a recital.
The girls wore dresses.
The boys wore suits.
Even Mommy and Daddy
were dressed up.
Grandpa wore a flower
in his buttonhole.

When it was Gus's turn,
he walked to the piano.
His tie was too long.
His shoes were too tight.
His heart was pounding.

He wished he could use
his music book.
But Mrs. Moore wanted him
to know his piece by heart.
She wanted her students
to have the music
in their fingers.

Gus got his fingers ready.
He hoped the music
was in them.
He made sure they were strong,
not squishy.

Gus started to play
"The Horse Race."
His horse was running along
as fast as it could.
Gus played the loud parts
very loud.
He played the soft parts
very soft.
He was close to the finish line!

Suddenly,
Gus couldn't remember the rest.
He sat still, trying to think.
No thoughts came.

Mrs. Moore handed him his music.
Gus finished the piece.

From across the room,
Grandpa gave Gus a proud smile.
Gus knew Grandpa thought
he had done pretty well,
all in all.

But Gus knew his horse
had lost the race again.

Family Band

Back at Gus's house,
Skipper was waiting.
He gave happy barks
when the family walked in.
Too bad there was no recital
for barking dogs.
Skipper would be
the best dog there.

"I brought something
  to show you,"
  Grandpa said to Gus.
  He went out to his car
  and returned with a black case.
  Inside the case
  was Grandpa's violin.

"You still have that old fiddle?"
  Daddy asked Grandpa.

"Don't you still have
  your old trombone?"
  Grandpa asked Daddy.

"It's around here somewhere,"
  Daddy said.

"Go find it,"
Grandpa told him.

Grandpa tuned his violin.
"I haven't played this thing
for forty years,"
he said to Gus.
"Let's see if I can still do it."

Grandpa picked up Gus's music.
He started to play it.
He made a couple of mistakes.
Gus grinned.

"Help me out," Grandpa said.

Gus started playing
"The Horse Race"
on the piano.
Grandpa started playing it
on the violin.

Daddy came back
and joined in with his trombone.
Mommy beat time
on a toy tambourine.
Skipper barked his loudest
opera barks.

They played "The Horse Race"
over and over again.
Soon their horse won every time!

Then Grandpa put down his bow.
"That's enough for these
old knuckles," Grandpa said.

"Just once more?"
Gus asked.
The music was in Gus's fingers now.

The doorbell rang.
It was Ryan Mason.
"You guys sound great!"
he said.

They played "The Horse Race"
one last time for Ryan.

"There's nothing like
being in a band,"
Grandpa said.
"Right, Skipper?"
Skipper gave a happy bark.

"I think Skipper likes bands
even better than opera,"
Gus said.
"I sure do."

And the band Gus liked best
was the one
with Gus and Grandpa in it.